Witch Way

Lester Tatum had a small problem. He inherited a bank account of more than three million dollars, but knew he couldn't use any lawyer within 150 kilometers of Kingston.

Could the local witch woman handle this kind of thing?

She was a lot of fun, and she was educated.

Worth a try!

Contents

About the author

CD Moulton has traveled extensively over much of the world both in the music business, where he was a rock guitarist, songwriter and arranger and in an import/export business. He has been everything from a bar owner to auto salvage (junkyard) manager, longshoreman to high steel worker, orchid grower to landscaper, tropical fish farmer to commercial fisherman. He started writing books in 1983 and has published more than 350 books as of January 1, 2023. His most popular books to date are about research with orchids, though much of his science fiction and fantasy work has proven popular. He wrote the CD Grimes, PI series, and the Det. Nick Storie series, Clint Faraday series, and many other works.

He now resides in Gualaca, Chiriqui, Panamá, where he writes books, plays music with friends, does research with orchids and medicinal plants. He has lately become involved in fighting for the rights of the indigenous people, who are among his closest friends, and in fighting the extreme corruption in the courts and police in Panamá.

He offers the free e-book, *Fading Paradise*, that explains what he has been through because of the corruption.

CD is the discoverer of the Chadam Protocol for curing cancer.

Facebook page Ambrosia peruviana for cancer.

Les Tatum snarled at the clock.

He would flush it, if it wasn't far enough from the bed that it would wake him up with its high-pitched screech. That was the only way it could get him out of bed. If he could reach it from there, he would knock it off the shelf and probably throw it across the room – or something.

He was the type that would stay in bed all day, if he could.

Well, maybe not. The way he had to piss would soon have him up.

He groaned, got up, and turned the alarm off.

He was tempted to get back in the bed.

Why was he wide awake as soon as the sun went down, and asleep on his feet as soon as it came up?

He'd been that way since he was about 8 years old. His [single] mother was the head barmaid in Goofy's Garden, all night bar/ restaurant on Coconut Street.

That was about two kilometers out of Kingston. It was a dump then, and it was a dump now.

An expensive dump.

Les was now the day manager. It was open 24 hours.

He didn't know anything else. His mother had tried, but that was what he learned, by induction. The school was too far away, and didn't turn out anybody prepared to live in a real place.

WTF good was algebra to a, face it, fancy bartender?

Social studies? Civics?

Great! He knew more or less what some of the politicians, like that bigshit senator, Lincoln Allen Peterson Carstairs the fourth, who were regulars [The cabins with the "girls" in back] were talking and joking about.

"She was after me like I was some movie star or something. She wouldn't leave me alone. Just like all those other women.

"I don't know what it is about me that makes them all want me to spend a couple of hours, discussing the way we need better trash pickup, wink, wink, wink.

"All the women seem to think all I have to do is give an order, and everything will be just peachy! They all think the best way to get me to change anything is in the bedroom! They drive me crazy!"

Then they pay fifty bucks for an hour in one of the cabins. Where are those two dozen women who just won't leave him alone?

Or they pay the fifty for a half hour with him.

What a mood! And he wouldn't even be there for more than an hour!

He lived in a cabin behind the "regular" ones. He saw them coming and going, all night, and most of the day.

Life sucks.

He giggled. So did a couple of them. He got enough propositions. He could make a few bucks, anytime he was hard up. He'd known that since he was ten years old, when that super-pious preacher gave him ten dollars to let him lick all over his body.

It felt sort of good. Word got around, and he made a lot of money at ten bucks a throw.

His mom found out about it, and said it had to stop – for ten bucks. Fifty was the going rate. No discounts.

Some of them wanted him to do things. He didn't think he'd like that. He told her. She said that was a hundred dollars.

He was now twenty two. 12 years, and he figured he'd made about a mil and a half for her.

She made a lot more than that, somehow. He didn't know how, until he was fifteen.

She was blackmailing a bunch of them. Because they went for him. He didn't learn it was against the law, as well as a way to get to hell when you died.

She told him to always keep it something they could afford. Get too greedy, and it comes apart, and you're in deep trouble.

Then she got greedy. He was eighteen when she was found, strangled, behind the Dumpster by the kitchen back door. Harry Lewis, the owner, made him head daytime bartender. That was a trade he knew better than anyone there, and he knew all the "special" customers.

Just last night, he found her bankbook. There was more than three million dollars – four years ago! It would be over five, by now, with the interest!

He had more than seventy grand in his own account.

He needed advice on how to claim that money. There was no one else [he knew about] in the family, and she didn't have a will, so it was automatically his. Even after the inheritance taxes, he would have more than three million.

He could live on that, for awhile.

And he could tell good old Harry to kiss his ass [That's fifty bucks!] with his crummy job!

He fixed some cinnamon pancakes, and had his regular large mug of coffee, showered and all that, put on some clothes that were more daytime, thought a few minutes about it, and went to work.

He was going to find how to get that money.

From things he'd learned at the bar since he was old enough to understand the words, there wasn't a lawyer within a hundred fifty kilometers he could trust out of his sight and hearing. They actually bragged to each other about how much they screwed [that's a hundred bucks!] client's out of.

Then who?

Mama Nani was supposed to make good things happen. She would be a lot cheaper than lawyers, and guarantees everything she does.

Would she take something about money?

She knew the law. She had even gone to university for two years to learn about it.

Did she know about banks?

One way to find out!

He took care of the stuff on his desk. Complaint because the chicken was raw. Tell cookie not to do that anymore, and give them a certificate for two complete meals, on the house. Belinda had not performed to the agreement ... that wasn't his department. He put it on Harry's spike. Nothing else he needed to take care of in any hurry.

"Neto! You're in charge for a little while. I have a couple of errands to take care of."

"Yo! Any reservations or that kind of shit?"

"For lunch [he checked the list], Andrews and Timkins on table six. Twelve thirty. Goodman and Castile, table four, from twelve. Lopez and Prinz at one. Table three.

"I should be back, but you can never tell! It's legal and bank shit, so it could take a week."

"Ain't *that* the truth!"

Mama Nani gave him a cup of tea. He grinned at her. She laughed.

"Forgot you know the schtick.

"Here."

She dumped the tea into a big fern and poured him a cup of the coffee she was drinking.

"So, Mon! What's you problem?"

"Mama Nani, it's me, Les."

"Yeah. I get into the tourist mode when I start. Had a rough night. Damned bitch thinks she can take my business.

"Les, I *do* have some power. She'd know that, if she had any.

"So! What's the pitch?"

"No pitch. I have about three million dollars in a bank account. Mom left it. I want it.

"Do you know anything about the banks here? What do I need to do?"

"They'll tax the holy shit out of you, but that shouldn't bother you, with that much.

"I took some economic classes. Banks are part of the system. They have some useful international laws. Depends on which bank, here."

"Kingston National."

"Hmmm. Not so good, from one end, very good, from another.

"Yveth died, what? Four years ago? They're just now notifying you?

"That's not legal. They have to contact you within thirty days, max. We can use that!"

"They didn't contact me. I found her bankbook."

"Then they planned to steal it. Probably already have.

"KN. Benicio Lezcano. Fat, French, Spanish, black. Nothing *proven* against him. The way he looks at all the little girls tells me there's something he wouldn't like to get out.

"He doesn't go to Goofy's, does he? The girls there are legal age."

"I don't think so. He's not a regular. I'd know the name."

"I'll see what I can do. He's the right mix he would fall for the voodoo bit.

"Maybe we can do it all legal. You *do* have the bankbook?"

"Yeah." He took it out of his pocket and handed it to her. She looked through it, and shook her head. "Bartenders make a shitload of money, don't they?"

He laughed. "Not if they're *only* a barmaid!"

She raised an eyebrow. "She sold me, since I

was eight – the old thing that I was ate before I was eight bit. She sold them silence, if you get the drift."

"So that would be why she was sliced up like bologna. I knew there had to be something."

"Yeah. I thought that – until night before last."

"What do you mean?"

"I thought it was because she tried to blackmail the wrong one, but found a bankbook that was supposed to be reported to me four years ago.

"It wasn't reported. It has literally millions in it.

"That opens up another set of possibilities, would you say?"

"I'd say something like that!"

"Okay. How much? What's the deal?"

"Hmm. How about five percent of what we collect?"

"Sounds good to me!"

"And a romp, now and then. You're gorgeous, and your reputation for bedroom sports precedes you!" She laughed, "I'm half serious!"

"I don't have a reputation with women. I was always sold to men.

"You know something? I think Mom made sure I wouldn't have any women. She was afraid I'd stop the whore bit, if I did."

"She was a real prize. Want to see if she was right?"

"I'll admit to some curiosity. I also have to say I don't feel much with sex."

She laughed. "Well, you have an offer! I'll bet you have hundreds of them that you turn down."

"I don't know about hundreds, but I was trained to turn down any offers that don't give me money."

"Come on! You've had offers from women, money included!"

"I don't know, before she was murdered. I've had some since. I ... just automatically turn them down. I think I'm afraid I'll like it, and that's bad for business."

"Well, what do you care about business, with a few million in the bank?"

"You have a point."

"Okay. Lezcano and Maria Estevez are the two who could work the scheme on you. She's his cousin, or something, and has been with that bank for sixteen years. Started as head of the loan department. A real tiger about foreclosing on valuable properties," Mama Nani said. "She's known to be a very religious person – but has not been known, for what I can find – to practice what she preaches, so to say.

"They both are big donors to their church. I'd say they're trying to buy their way into heaven."

"Did you get anything about the account?"

"I sent a normal type of query about it, and suggested an heir was asking if such existed. Please remit an accounting of any such accounts extant.

"I'm registered in the Bahamas as an accountant and lawyer. That will make them think there's another worm in their big shiny apple. Maybe one they can't directly reach.

"Did you enjoy last night as much as I did, and you seemed to?

"It was different. I think I really did enjoy it. None of the physical feelings were what I expected."

They finished their breakfast. Les decided he'd go to work, like usual. Maybe they'd not connect him with anything.

Harry seemed curious about where he was yesterday. There were no problems, but he was needed at his station, at times.

"I had some things come up with relatives I didn't even know I had. In the Bahamas. Apparently, my father was from there.

"They want a DNA test! I don't know what that would prove."

"It would prove their choice of your father is or isn't true."

"But, so what?" Les tried to look totally confused. "If they think they can get some kind of inheritance or something, there wasn't much of anything."

"Oh, they're trying to find out if she had a big bank account, or, er, something, I guess.

"Well, it's no concern of mine!

"Do we need more Chivas and Tanqueray? Neto said we're low."

"We have a couple cases in the storeroom. I'll check it out."

Harry nodded, and went to his office.

I wonder how the fuck you even knew about that bit! Harry, I think you need a little investigation, yourself!

He went to the stockroom, checked the items on the inventory lists, wrote a purchase order for a few things, and called Mama Nani.

"Why did Harry know about my relatives in the Bahamas?"

"He did?

"Uh-huh."

"The thot plickens!"

"Nan, I think I want to find ... if Mom had a safe deposit box at that bank!"

"I thought about that. Where did she keep the blackmail evidence?

"She didn't have one in that bank.

"Did she ever take you to any other bank that you remember?"

"All of them here, once or tw ... And did she have other accounts? I knew about this one because my account's here."

"Methinks this one might get hairy! Methinks every bank here is going to get the query letter. Registered with the court system, with a little hint or two.

"Les, I think Harry is either part of it, is running the scam, or suddenly has his fat ass in a crack.

"Methinks a declaration from the superior court that all accounts or other use of facilities are to be opened to the heir and his lawyer, immediately, complete with all records concerned in the matter. Not complying, fully, could well result in charges brought because standard legal notification was not complied with in the time blah, blah, blah."

"Nan, it could get damned dangerous."

"Oh, it is that, already. I do have some power. I can sense, instantly, when someone wants to attack me. I think I can expand it to where I'll know if they plan to attack you. I can sense what kind of attack.

"Les, you go to work in the morning at your regular time, and keep up the stupid ignorant victim act. Keep them off guard.

"Is there some time when you know Harry will be there? I can just happen to pick that time to deliver a copy of the court order to you."

"A real court order?"

"Uh-huh. Judge Larue is a client for some things.

"It'll bring the court into it, so will cost you about five percent in court costs – that Louis will put in his pocket."

"Seems a good enough deal.

"Harry is always there at ten, when the shift changes."

"I'll time it for that. See you at ten in the morning. At Goofy's."

"Oh, Les, is that bank account thing making any progress?" Harry asked, innocently. He had met Les at the loading dock platform, where "The Senator" was just leaving in his taxpayer-funded limousine.

"Bank thing? I have my account, and nobody can touch that, because it doesn't have anything to do with any inheritance. She only left three thousand dollars in the house, and that was almost all used up in the funeral."

"I mean the Bahama people, or whatever."

"Oh, Mama Nani is in that, somehow. She had me sign a thing so she could get something from someone. I don't even try to understand what banks are about.

"Speak of the devil! Hi, Mama Nani! We were

just talking about you!" Nani came in the front door, just then. Harry spun around [not easy for someone that fat] and looked trapped.

"About me? I didn't do nothin' to you, Mon! Just got this here court order to all the banks here. Some city lawyer said somethin' 'n the judge said it be corruption, and they's gonna investigate all'n'em.

"I can drop the act. Harry knows it ain't the real me, much as you.

"Did Yveth tell you about her accounts? Did the bank send you a registered letter, or come to see you in person, within thirty days of the funeral?"

"I didn't hear anything from any bank, but ... you mean, did I know she had an account?

"I guess so, but I doubt there was anything in it. Mom always said she had a lot of expenses, and could never get ahead, even a hundred dollars. Even when she made two or three hundred from my stuff, she was always two dollars from being broke."

"Your stuff? I don't ... oh. It's true? You were having sex with that bunch of cruds for money?"

"Yeah. Everybody knows that! I made four hundred fifty dollars in one night, when I was eleven, but ... shit!

"She was putting all that in the bank? She just pretended to be broke?

"If there is anything in the bank, it's mine! I earned it!"

"That's why I got the government and court in it. They were supposed to notify you right away, and didn't."

Harry was sweating. Profusely. "How did you, a wit ... er, medicine woman, get any court order?"

"I got a license. I went to college. The witch bit is for entertainment, and I *do* have powers.

"Les, I have the demands to deliver. Can you take a few minutes off work and go with me to deliver them?

"You are the plaintiff, so it gets past some things if you're present."

"Well, I took off a couple of days ago, so I don't know if ... Is it okay, Harry?"

"Er, ghee, I can't ... there isn't time to ... that is."

"Well, I would think you'd be glad your faithful employee might get a break, myself!" Nani snarled.

"Why, of course. I just meant, we have to have someone ... maybe Neto?"

"I can ask him," Les said. "He hasn't left yet, and he's on for a couple hours, so it shouldn't take longer than that?"

"Depends on what we run up on at the banks. It shouldn't take more than ten minutes at any of them. Just deliver the court order."

"Er, all of them?" Harry asked, in a squeak.

"We don't know how many accounts she had," Nani said.

"Ghee!" Harry was about to faint. Nani grinned at Les, and winked.

"Well, I'll get Neto, and we can get it over with. I hope Mom had enough to where I can get some new clothes, and like that. If she was putting what I made in the bank, there should be five thousand, at least!"

He waved at Harry, and went to the kitchen to tell Neto he would be gone for awhile. Harry looked like he was sick, or something. Maybe the flu going around.

Neto grinned. "I could hear a little of it. He was stealing, all along?

"I've heard stories, and I've seen some things."

"Be careful. He has some scary friends that are supposed to be with the cartels. Don't let anyone know you even suspect anything. He even has a senator who has some kind of deal with him."

"Yeah. I ain't that stupid."

Les waved, told Harry Neto was good with it. He'd get back as soon as he could.

He and Nani left.

"You ain't coming back here. I saw his plan, clear! He's on the phone, right now, trying to get a hit man to arrange an accident for you and me.

"I'll know if he's able to set something up. We can not be where he wants us to be when he wants us to be there."

Les looked grim, and nodded.

"This is Mr. Hargraves, our head of legal matters. He can advise us about this order, and ascertain if it is, indeed, a legal document," Chavez Grantly, CEO of the national bank, said, looking down his nose at them. Mr. Lezcano will arrive soon, and he can decide if we will give you any information at all."

Nani shrugged. "It's a court order from the superior court. You can comply, or warm a cell until someone else complies. They can also be incarcerated for contempt of a court order.

"I thought this was just some greedy people in the Bahamas who were trying to work a scam. Your reaction tells me it isn't all them in on the scam.

"Mr. Tatum, I can think of only one reason we are meeting with this strange resistance to following a simple, standard court order. Just failing to notify you could be waved away as an oversight, or as something that happened because she didn't fill out a form, or something – though we all know perfectly well that she *did* fill out the form.

"Tell Lezcano I'll be back, later. I can bring a police officer, if that becomes necessary.

"Mr. Tatum, we have to get to the Shore Trust, then can go to the Ringold Savings and Loan, then District Five, then return here. If we get this bullshit line from the others, I'll bring a couple of people from the TV and other media. They can ask why, if you have nothing to hide.

"We should be back in about an hour and a half."

They went out, through the lobby, and to a cab that was just sitting there. Nani slapped her head and said they forgot to get the signature on form three. They went back inside. Nani said, "If we got in that cab, we would never arrive. Anywhere."

"And that could only have been set up with Harry," Les said. "You live and learn – or you die.

"What now?"

They waited a few minutes, then went back out. The cab was still there. Another was being flagged down by a woman.

"Gee! I wonder why she didn't take the one just sitting there!" Nani said. "It's just two blocks. We'll walk."

They headed the other way. The cab started up, came alongside, and tooted the horn. Nani wagged her finger, "No. I know how to flag a damned taxi! It's the same, anywhere in the world!"

They went on. The cab turned the corner ahead, toward the Shore Trust building.

"Gee! I said Shore Trust, when I meant Ringold!" Nani said, They turned the other way at the corner. As they were stepping off the curb to cross the street, Nani grabbed Les's arm and pulled him back, as the taxi hurtled by, almost running over the curb onto the sidewalk.

"Guy has the worst luck!" Nani said. Three people came running up. Les said they should put the driver in that cab away for ten years for operating a vehicle under the effects of drugs, or something!

They turned around, and headed for Shore Trust.

"I'm getting pretty good at seeing when those cruds are planning something.

"Les, I got a flash, then. The driver's name is LeSeur. Bryan LeSeur."

"Maybe we can cause the poor incompetent idiot a bit of trouble.

"Did you see that anonymous woman who saw it, recognized the driver from when she was ... where?"

Nani looked intensely thoughtful for a few seconds. "New Orleans. In the states.

"I think, seeing that police officer right over

there saw it, that we should make a formal complaint. The anonymous caller can call a few minutes after!”

They both laughed. Les waved at the cop, who came over to them,.

“You were really lucky that idiot didn’t hit you! I called in the cab number, so we’ll get him!”

“Well, officer. I wouldn’t think much about it, the way some people insist on drinking and driving, but it was a taxi! It was the same one that tried to get us to take it at the bank, but we’re not taking any cab to go three blocks!” Nani said.

“You say that same taxi tried to ... just a sec.” His walky-talky said there was no cab of that number registered.

“I don’t know what’s going on anymore!” Nani cried. “You mean he tried to deliberately hit us?! *Why*?”

“We’ll try to find him,” the cop promised.

“Well, we have to get to the bank. I’m getting scared to cross the street!” Nani said, indignantly. They walked away.

Les took out his cell phone and called the police. He used a squeaky voice that sounded like an old woman. He reported that she saw a cab try to deliberately hit a young man and woman, and she was from the states, and she knew the very one who was driving the cab, from New Orleans, where he was a hood with the mafia, or something. His name was Bryan LeSeur." He rang off.

"All incoming calls are recorded. Should be interesting!" he said.

They went to the bank, where much the same thing happened as with National, then Ringold, where the man checked over all the accounts, right there, and said there was no account there in that name.

Then to the last one, who said there was an account there in that name, but as part of a corporation. An S.A. GoFlyHard. She was listed as secretary/treasurer. He couldn't give anymore information.

Ringold had no such account there.

Then back to National, where Lezcano almost fainted when they walked into his office.

"It can be dangerous crossing the street here!" Nani said. "Good thing I've learned to look both ways before crossing. We could have been killed!

"Well! No harm done!

"Now, about the account?"

"There is no such account here," Lezcano said, haughtily. "Please leave the premises, or I will be forced to have you expelled!"

Les tossed the bankbook copy onto the desk."

"Oh, fuck!" Lezcano cried. "I mean, we don't seem to have any record that would indicate ...

that is, we have looked over our files, and didn't find ... I assure you, we will investigate this, thoroughly!"

"The government will do the investigating. Here and Shore.

"You might just wonder where the lovely lady had other little, shall we say, embarrassing items secreted for her son to find.

"And who else is implicated."

"I'll bring a certificate of death and withdraw my funds from your bank.

"Now! About the safety deposit bit!"

"She didn't have any such thing here!" Lezcano said, tiredly.

"But GoFlyHard does," Nani said.

He looked surprised. He looked through the computer list, and said, "I'll be damned! Right here, under our noses, and we never saw it or connected ... so who was working that part?"

"Do you think she could pull off that kind of thing where her boss wouldn't know something was fishy?" Les asked.

"But he's a partn ... God! I can be so stupid!"

"No argument there!" Les agreed.

"Well, we can handled this, as you would say, 'discreetly' – or not," Nani suggested. "We'll make a little deal. I'm against blackmail, all the way – except for a few things. Like harming innocent people.

"Here's the death certificate and the court declaration that Les, Mr. Tatum, is legal heir to all assets of the deceased.

"Shall we peruse the contents of a safedeposit box or three?"

A rather sever looking shapely woman charged into the room, yelling, "Benicio! Don't answer any questions! Do not talk to these people!"

"Ah! The lovely Maria!" Nani greeted. "I'm afraid the talking is already mostly done. It's action time.

"Care to accompany us to the vault?"

"Er, uh, what?"

"The box is right here, in this bank," Lezcano said, tiredly. "Seems there were others in her end of it. At least one of them was playing us."

"Who? I can ... No one could be doing that! We would *know*!"

"Really? Why would my boss know anything about it, then?" Les asked, innocently.

"Fuck!" Maria spat. "We can make a deal!"

"Just what I already suggested," Nani said.

"What kind of deal?" Lezcano asked.

"I get what is rightfully mine," Les said. "Beyond that, it will depend on what's in the boxes, and who was working it on me, and how."

"It was set up with Harry, about ten years ago,"

Lezcano replied. "He had set it up with Yveth for the blackmail thing. He did that when he got the pictures and IDs of people with you and the other girls at Goofy's. Most of the politicians and business people use the facilities at Goofy's, from, time to time.

"Mr. Tatum, I didn't know about you until she died. I wouldn't have gone along with that. I like younger women, but not less than thirteen or so. You were about ten years old when she started that, weren't you?"

"Eight. I don't think it's hurt me. It would hurt kids who were raised differently."

"Well, to the vault. We'll see what happens," Maria said. "I really want to see if she actually had what she said about me."

"It may be in another bank, since you're right here, and you could probably find a way to get it, if you found out about the box," Nani said.

"Other bank?" she asked.

"The Shores, at least. And Ringold," Nani replied.

"Shit!"

"We'll get it all. We'll stick by our end, so long as you stick by yours. Harry will *not* get away with anything."

"A particular reason?" Lezcano asked.

"He hired a hit on us that failed," Les answered.

"I sort of get pissed off about that kind of thing.

"Not about the 'failed' part."

"I reckon!"

They found the box and were able to open it, after getting a lot of paperwork and bringing in the bank's own locksmith. It took two keys, one from the bank, and one from the boxholder, which they didn't have.

Maria had looked thoughtful, and had checked the records. Harry had been there four times, so he had the other key.

Most of what was there was photos, with notes about the date and time, and the names of the people in the pictures. There were several memory sticks. Nani took the pictures, dropped them into the shredder, and turned it on, then ran the scraps through a second time.

"Oops! I dropped the evidence! Did anyone see where it went?"

They all laughed.

They then went back to the main office, where Lezcano filled out a form that was in his personal safe. A form that was stamped as registered four years ago. It added Leter Tatum's name as co-holder of the account, and stated that, in event of death or disability, the account had automatically reverted to the survivor.

"Rights of survivor," Maria explained. "No

inheritance taxes, because it was already yours, so we didn't have to file on it for you.

"Now! Let's see what's on those memory sticks!"

They used the computer on her desk. Most of it was borderline, and would cause a politician or government worker – or priests and preachers – to lose their jobs and be disgraced.

"Those last two, and a couple of others, deserve being crucified!" Nani said. "We'll let it go, but on the agreement that we will all try to get them caught if they ever do anything like that again!"

She formatted the memory stick, then crushed it with the marble inkstand and dropped it into the wastepaper basket.

The second was much the same. The third was a bit more, but they would have to produce the whole thing for any of it to be prosecuted, so it got the same ending.

"Well, that shit was purely disgusting!" Nani declared. "There was nothing about you two, but we met that Hargraves SOB here. I take it you will let him know you found out about him and those six year old twins, in your own way."

"He was a minor player. He knew they had something on him, but not what, according to him," Lezcano said. "We will soon have a short discussion, and he will be seeking other gainful employment. Without recommendation."

"Well, did you know of the other accounts?" Nani asked.

"I knew of the Shores account, but not about the box," Maria said. "You realize that Guerra has to know about the box there. Perhaps he will have already opened it. He's the type to try the blackmail angle if he thought he would get away with it.

"I think he wouldn't have found it, if he hadn't."

"Seeing we've gone this far, maybe I can use the bank's links to discover a few things about this case," Lezcano suggested. "Maria, go to code 'GLUE' and access 'orilla.'

"That's a world bank code to get us into the records of Shore. We can go there as a group and put some pressure on them, if we have damning information.

"Same as Mama Nani did to us."

"We can give it the old college try!" Les said, and laughed.

It took the better part of an hour, but they traced another account there that also had more than three million dollars in it.

"I don't know how we can use this, because we can be accused of hacking," Lezcano complained. "If we can force them to open a specific account, we have them, and they won't dare to fight you.

"I have to seem scared of what you found about me."

"I done got a real good recall 'bout numbers, Mon!" Mama Nani said. "I done got you tight 'cause Mama Nani ain't never wrong 'bout no numbers! If she there, she know! She tell you, Mon! You done got to buy a shot of rum for Mama Nani, cause she done got you a favor!

"I does have the power, Mon!"

"Worth a try!" Maria exclaimed. "Guerra is a little ratfaced snake. He'll believe in that kind of thing. He's running scared all the time, and you can make it look like his fears have caught up with him!

"I'll get a real kick out of watching that worm squirm!"

They told the main office they would be away for the rest of the afternoon, so would take any appointments tomorrow. It was less than an hour to closing, so wouldn't be a great inconvenience.

They stopped at a little restaurant for a quick meal, then got to Shore ten minutes before closing. Guerra saw them coming in, and looked confused, then scared, then defiant.

"We'll need a few minutes of your time for a conference on banking practices, or something," Maria announced.

"I'm afraid I can't spare the time today. Perhaps

tomorrow at nine thirty?"

"You ain't got no appointment a tall!" Mama Nani snarled. "You done got caught out! You gone be in jail tomorrow by nine, you doan save you rotten soul afore then!"

"Who are you? What?!"

"I called Mama Nani, 'n June three, just afore midnight, two year past, you done sold you ass to the devil, 'n you got no way out ceptin me!"

"Wheee! Er, June ... what are you ranting about?!"

"You go close you bank, 'n you comes right back here, 'n we talks a bit!"

He looked around at each of them. Nani was staring at him in a way that scared even Les, who knew it was an act.

Guerra went to the lobby and the head teller's station.

"I heard something about a little boy who drowned then, and got a flash," Nani explained. "Sometimes they're true, sometimes they're not. This one, as you may have noted, is true.

"Go along with me. The flash says we get what we want, and that he's dead before morning. He's going to go swimming where he killed that seven year old boy.

"I'm confused at what else was there. It was hints, but they're gone, now, and I can't bring them back before their time."

They agreed. After about ten minutes, Guerra came back. "Okay. We'll talk in my office, but you better not be ... you have to explain what you're trying to say."

They went into the office. Guerra went to behind the desk, Maria and Lezcano sat on the over-stuffed sofa, Lester went to sit on the stool by the secretary's desk, and Mama Nani stood in front of Guerra.

"What's this stuff about, when was it? June?"

Mama Nani's eyes rolled back, and her voice seemed to come from somewhere behind her. "I'm Billy! I'm gonna tell! You aren't supposed to do that! I'm gonna tell!" Then sounds of water and gurgling, [How did she do that?] then her face relaxed, and she was staring blankly at the ceiling.

She shook her head. "What I done said, Mon?"

"Billy? Who's Billy?" Les asked.

"Billy? What you say, Mon? Bi ... [her face went hard, there were tears running down her cheeks.] 'He killed me! He raped me and killed me! I'm Billy Williams!' ... lly was ... seven? ... What I done said, Mon?"

"That Guerra raped and killed a seven year old boy on June 3, two years ago," Maria said. "I think we can find out just where from police records. They'll have DNA samples, I'm sure.

"You are going to be strapped onto a cot and you are going to receive a little injection, bastard!"

Guerra was sobbing. "I didn't mean it! I couldn't stop!"

"You done can open the safe box and give this here Lester what's rightfully his!" Mama Nani said. "Then we give you four hours to get from here 'afore we's tellin the police!"

"I swear! I don't know what account you mean! I only know about the box! I'll open it! There's nothing in it! I burned everything!"

"That done be true.

"What you say? What Billy? He done gone 'n help Mama Nani. I can call him, now he done called me."

"Billy Williams. He died two years ago," Maria said. "I never believed this stuff! I *saw* it, right here!"

Mama Nani got a strange look on her face. "Billy Williams? You done got a ... number fo Mama Nani?"

Her eyes rolled back. The voice came from, seemingly, behind Guerra, who spun and almost turned his chair over. There was nobody there.

Lester grabbed a pen and some paper from the desk.

"Billy, Bob. Bert, Andy, Alex, Alan, two, seven, nine, seven, zero, hyphen, four, four, seven, one, two, two, Mark, Mitch, Manny, hyphen, two Fred."

Mama Nani relaxed, and asked, "You done wrote it down, Mon?"

"Yeah, Mama Nani," Les replied. "Guerra, you open that computer and find that account. Now!"

Guerra took the paper and typed at the computer. An account came up. It had three million dollars and change in it. It was a holding account, like an open-ended escrow account.

In the name of Lester Evan Tatum.

"Cripes! We never thought to look for something in *my* name!"

They all [except Guerra] laughed.

Guerra called in a department head and had a bankbook issued to Les. They all left. Nani went back to the office door, and said, "You done got fo hours."

They left.

"Well, that ties it up," Maria said. "I think it's best, for all of us, if we let this dog lie until it dies."

"So long as it stops here, I'll agree," Nani said. Lester and Lezcano nodded.

They split up. Nani and Les headed for his cabin.

Nani stopped him. "I don't think it would be a good idea to go back to where a person who tried to hire a hit on us is."

He agreed with that! "And we still have the killer of my Mom to expose."
"There is that."

"How are we going to catch him in a way that's legal?" Les asked. "We can use what we have, and can show there's no other way it could be, but a court will throw it out, with a few dollars consideration to the judge."

"The police didn't find LeSeur. We could have broken him down fairly fast."

"We do have one thing that ... he had access to that safe deposit box. There were nine million bucks we know about involved, three of which were already in my name."

"And, even if they could get around not notifying about the other accounts, they can't get around not sending you a financial report on an escrow account every quarter. Once per year, they have to get your signature on a continuance."

"All of which adds up to zilch, so far as Harry is concerned."

"I think I'll go calling on Harry. I think he'll have to explain why he knew all about the accounts – and why he tried to have us killed."

"No, Nan. It's too dangerous."

"I can handle it. It's got to be done at the right

time and in the right place.

"I'll try a little psychology. My talent will tell me if it's working.

"He's calling you, right now! He's scared shitless by this!"

Les's cell phone buzzed. He grinned at Nani, and answered, "Hi, Harry! What's the haps?"

"Hi, Les. We need you here! There's a big crowd tonight, and Neto is coming in, but the setup is behind. You're the expert on that!"

Nani shook her head.

"I can try to get away from this mess ... who's there? Marta?"

"Er, uh, yeah. She's getting things tangled. She doesn't know how to do anything without instructions."

Nani winked, and signed to get her on the phone.

"Can you put her on? I can see she does a few things to make it a lot easier."

"Uh, she's not ... she's in the kitchen."

"That's where she should be. Let me talk to her. I can straighten most of it out until I can get there.

"We found nine million dollars in accounts that all belong to me! I'm with lawyers and all that. Taxes on part of it, you know."

He winked at Nani.

"You know it was against international law for them not to tell me about it within thirty days? I can sue them for fifty million more, on just what I've got, so far!"

"World bank investigation!" Nani said with the voice-throwing trick.

"What was that?!" Harry cried.

"Some guys from Interpol, or something. What?"

Nani used the trick to say, just barely audibly, "We're World Bank investigators. You are Lester Tatum?"

"Uh, yes?

"Tell Marta to set up like we did for that big birthday party two weeks ago, Harry. Talk later." He rang off.

"He's shitting his pants!" Nani said, laughing. "He had it all set up where LeSeur could back a truck up and crush you against that wall by the loading dock. He's almost in a panic because of us World Bank investigators.

"I think I'm gonna greatly enjoy watching that piece of shit squirm.

"Gimme your phone. Put the privacy call on."

He looked a question at her, and put the phone on "hide caller ID" before handing it to her.

She punched the emergency code/police, and waited a few seconds, then used the old woman voice.

"I called earlier about those young people who

that LeSeur person tried to run down. I see he is at this restaurant, right now.

"Why?"

"In the back. I saw him when I went to the restroom. Why is he not locked up?"

"They call it a goofy restaurant, or something."

"I'm here. If it becomes necessary, I will speak with your officers." She rang off.

"They're sending a unit to Goofy's. I think maybe I'll just happen to be there when the police raid the place.

"Harry's going to soon think he was dead wrong when he thought his luck was at the worst it possibly could be!"

They did a high five.

"Do you think they'll be able to tag LeSeur? Will he be there?"

"He's sitting in the truck that's supposed to back into you."

"How is Harry planning to get me back there?"

"He's going to have a drink with you to celebrate your good fortune. He can then walk you to the right spot and tell you to stand there until he gets back. You won't resist in any way."

"You can see that much?"

"Yeah. I done got a concentration spell on you, Mon! Anybody tries to hurt you, I knows! All'n it!

"Maria is plotting to get her hands on at least half of your great good fortune. She'll seduce you, marry you, then knock you off, after a couple of months. Failing that, she'll divorce you and get half!"

"We know the loveliest people!"

They laughed.

"Well, I'd better get over to Goofy's to accidentally be passing when the place gets a truckload of cops running around with their AK-forty sevens."

"Maybe I'll get to work about fifteen minutes later?"

She looked thoughtful, then an impish grin spread across her face. "As I said, Harry's bad luck is going to get into the impossibly horrible stage!"

They kissed passionately, then Nani went to the restaurant. Les cleaned up and changed clothes, and headed for the restaurant. Just as he went out the door, he heard shots, two from a pistol, and a lot from a machine gun. From the direction of Goofy's Restaurant.

When he got to the restaurant, there was an ambulance, a police truck, four policemen wandering around, and Harry, sitting in a chair by the kitchen entrance. Two medics were loading a fifth policeman into the ambulance on a Gurney. There was a body bag, obviously occupied, by the delivery truck at the loading dock.

"Who are you, and what are you doing here?" a cop asked, with his hand on his sidearm. "ID?"

"Lester Tatum. I work here." He handed the cop his ID card.

"What's going on? I heard shots!"

"A fugitive, wanted for attempted murder, here, and two murders in the states. He shot Genio. We shot back, with better aim. Genio isn't too badly hurt.

"Did you know the suspect?"

"Until I know who he was, I couldn't say."

"Oh. Some guy from the states. LeSeur something."

"We use LeSeur early peas in the restaurant. That's the only LeSeur I know anything about."

"Well, we'll clear this up as soon as we can. Probably won't be a good night for business."

Les nodded, then went to the kitchen entrance to ask Harry what the fuck was going on, now? Harry smirked and shrugged. Nani came from inside, and over to them. The cop came to them.

"Les, Mr. Tatum, it was that person who tried to hit us with the taxi!" Nani cried. "A woman, a Beatrice Albright, said she saw that, and recognized me, and asked if you were alright.

"She said she called the police, because she called earlier, and he was here, when he should be in jail.

"I didn't know what the hell she was talking about, but, you see what it was about.

"She said the dead man was talking to Harry, earlier, then he was back here, so she called the police to give them a piece of her mind about letting a cheap mafia thug run around the streets, trying to hit people with a car."

"Ma'am, can you introduce me to the lady? We will have to speak with her," the cop said.

"She was upset when she heard the guns, and left. I think she said it was time she got to the boat and they found a more tranquil kind of place to spend her money."

"Well, we want to thank her for the information. I guess we won't need more. We have the recordings from the emergency line.

"Can you describe her?"

"Sort of ordinary. Maybe five four, thin, grey hair, wore glasses.

"I don't know. Very expensive jewelry. A real emerald pendant with diamonds around. Sort of sour looking.

"I felt she was used to a lot of attention, used to be a beauty, wasn't anymore, and was sour about it."

"Well, sounds like a lot of those rich people who usually hang around the marina. 'Out slumming,' as they call it. Had a limousine in front to take her back after her little adventure."

"I didn't see any limousine when I came in. There was a Lexus, or one of those. Out by the road."

"Well, thank you, Ma'am. I've seen you around the area. You are a medical doctor?"

"No. I give out a little natural medicine, at times. Some of them are better than the drug store crap."

"Ain't it the truth! Thanks!" He went back to where they were loading the body bag into the police truck.

"Well!" Harry said, looking smug, "We do have a little excitement, at times!

"The Albright woman saw me talking with the dead guy? I don't remember that, but I greet a lot of people I don't remember. Part of owning a bar and restaurant.

"Les, Marta has the room usable, but not the way I want it – but I suppose the party won't happen, anyway, now."

"I just came by to get my junk from the cabin. I would quit tomorrow. I have nine million dollars, so I'm damned well not going to stay a bartender!"

"You won't have any nine million dollars!" Nani said "After taxes, you'll only have about seven and a half."

"I can just squeak by with that!

"I wonder if Mom left anything else. There are several safe deposit boxes we have to check out."

"Er, several safe...?" Harry asked, looking a little scared. "I know she had two, and that one was empt ... you see, Donnie Gooden was at the bank, and told me about it. His boyfriend works at the bank, and was all excited about it."

Nani was just behind him, and was having trouble not laughing out loud.

"There are a couple more. The one had a lot of stuff I think she was using to blackmail people. Politicians, mostly. And preachers. That's the only way I can explain the millions."

"Les, that Guerra person said something that I'm wondering about," Nani said. "You remember? He said *she* didn't use the box much, but someone else had accessed it a lot, according to their records.

"I was distracted, and it went over my head.

"We have to find out who. It could explain a lot of things.

"Did she have some kind of partner in the blackmail?"

"That would be stupid beyond belief!" Les cried. "A *partner* in blackmail? A partner who she trusted, and who trusted her?

"How idiotic! What they were doing would tell

exactly how much they could be trusted! It would never work!

"Unless ... maybe the partner was doing a little blackmail on her? A way to keep a name out of it, if they were caught?"

"My thoughts, exactly!"

"And that would explain her murder," Les said, pretending to be thinking deeply. "The only way to keep that name out would be to get rid of the person who could bring it out."

"And that person will be named in another box. Probably is named as the one who accessed the empty box."

Harry was sweating again, profusely.

"I think we'd better call on friend Guerra in the morning, if he hasn'r skipped out on us. He has to know he's in an impossible situation," Nani suggested. "It'll be easier and faster than checking the bank records with another court order."

"I think we can get that investigator to get us the information without any trouble," Les replied. "Somebody's ass is going to be in boiling oil over that one!"

"Well, I hope you get him!" Harry said. "It just gets deeper and deeper. Me, I would just take the money and run, so to speak. A world cruise, and no worries. Keep digging, and keep getting in deeper and deeper, until your time isn't yours, anymore!

"I better see everything's ready if the party does show up."

He went back through the kitchen and into the restaurant.

Nani said, "I thought he'd die of a heart attack, right here!"

"You know something, Nan? I think he enjoyed that LeSeur is dead a bit too much, don't you?"

"What do you mean?"

"He could see LeSeur wasn't going to succeed at anything. LeSeur knew too much. Some woman had seen the earlier attempt to knock us over, and had reported it, so success with this one would mean, eighty percent, that he would be caught, and would make any deal he could to survive – such as telling them who hired him.

"He knew LeSeur would try to shoot his way out of being caught. Ninety percent, he would get shot trying. He had a handgun, the police have AK-forty sevens.

"The bad part, to him, was that he didn't take me out, first. Some old woman recognized him and had the police raid the place.

"Okay. That could work out alright. I'm stupid as dirt, and didn't even suspect him of anything.

"Then some banker ass mentioned that Mom wasn't the one who was using a safedeposit box.

He could have the banker hit – but his hit man was dead! There's an investigation by the World Bank! They'll get the bank records! His name is on the access list!

"His ass is back in, tighter than ever!"

Nani laughed. "To top it off, some local witch was contacted, and knew every detail!"

Nani froze. "Let's get the hell out of here! He has nothing more to lose, and knows it! We're safe in two minutes if we can be far enough from this place!"

They dodged out the back door and ran for the road.

There was an explosion in the restaurant kitchen. They would have been smeared all over the back lot if they were still in that doorway. It knocked them off their feet at a hundred fifty feet away.

"Blew the big propane tank right by where we were talking. He was in the front, and didn't know we weren't there, anymore.

"Give me your phone."

Les handed her his phone. She punched Harry's number on fast-dial.

He answered with, "What? There's been some kind of explosion in the kitchen!"

"I knows. I is got the power. You gone to hell, soon."

She shut the phone off. "Now he's got to get us

both before we can get to the police.”

"I think, just maybe, the safest place for us right now is Goofy’s Bar and Restaurant.

"Would Mama Nani like a nice cool little rum and coke?”

"If the bar’s open, that done sound fetchin’!”

They did a high five.

There were two fire trucks just pulling onto the parking lot. There were three ambulances going around back, along with a police cruiser.

They went into the bar, where Neto was cleaning up dozens of broken glasses.

"Wow! The place blew up in back! Harry's going crazy! Both cooks are dead, and Marta!" Neto cried. "I'm lucky I was in the beer cooler room, or I'd be dead, too!

"Harry said to let him know if you came in, but that was before that goon was shot in back!

"Now, *this* is one night I'll never forget!"

"We were talking with Harry, not five minutes before the explosion," Les said. "We had left, and were just out by the road.

"I think I need a drink.

"You know Mama Nani?"

"I've seen her around. I'm Neto. Les is my boss."

"Rum and coke, tall. Two.

"I *was* your boss. I got an inheritance, and we were here to tell Harry I quit. He seemed to be upset because I inherited millions of dollars.

"That seemed strange. If any of my friends or co-workers inherited a lot, I'd be happy for them."

"Harry's always been strange. It's just the last few days he seems completely nuts," Neto replied. "I think all the bad luck is his own doing. He forgets to order stuff, it isn't here, and it's my fault, or yours, or Cookie's. 'The Senator' was here earlier, and was reading him the riot act about something. I think it was about you and your cabin, and when ... oh! Sorry."

Nani said, "He's a club whore. I know all about it. He's still the hottest stud I've ever come across."

They all laughed.

"Carstairs was ranting about me?" Les asked. "I mean, about what? Because he's gay?"

"I think about something that happened eight or ten years ago. Something Yveth was involved with."

"Oh. Because I was just twelve years old. He should know I'll never tell anyone about it. He was just a cheap lawyer, then. He's only been a senator nine years."

"You just told me about it."

"No, he told you about it. Seeing you already knew, what's the big deal?"

Neto handed them the drinks. They chatted awhile. Neto finished cleaning up the bar area, the fire trucks and ambulances left, and a policeman came in to stare at them.

"How long ... I mean, how long have you been here?"

"I never left, except to see Gene and Yvonne and Marta were dead. I looked in the restaurant, but there was so much yelling and running around I came back here to clean the place up," Neto said. "Les and Mama Nani came in about five or ten minutes later. They were here just before the blast, and came back to check on everybody."

"Christ! How did you survive that blast, this close?"

"I was in the cool room. I didn't even hear much. The insulation, you know. I felt a little pressure, like someone slammed the door hard."

"You just came in and started picking up the broken glass? Just like that?"

"I would only be in the way out there. I don't know what to do in that kind of thing, and nobody seemed to need more help.

"To tell the truth, I didn't know what I was supposed to do, so I just did my job."

"And you two just came in to have a drink, with all that?" He was staring in disbelief.

"We needed a drink," Nani said. "We were talking to Harry ten feet from that tank, not five minutes before it blew!"

"Harry? Who ... oh. The owner.

"I'm not supposed to tell you, but that tank had a bomb taped to one side, behind, and was set off with a radio control of some kind.

"A known criminal was shot just outside, earlier.

"I can add. The thug was here to rig that tank. It was supposed to kill Harry, the owner. You were lucky that it didn't go off a few minutes earlier!"

"That could very well be," Les said. "Only ... well, the hood was dead. Who set it off? Was it on some kind of timer?

"How? A timer couldn't tell when Harry was back there."

"Yeah. We'll have to work it out," the cop said. "Tell you the truth, thanks for not going out there and yelling at us for not stopping it before it happened. Like, we could have stopped something we never had a clue was going on?"

"People, as a group, are stupid," Les said. The cop grinned, and left.

"Well, there's nothing we can do here," Nani said. "Let's go get your stuff from the cabin and go to my place."

Les looked at her. She nodded ever so slightly. They said their goodbyes to Neto, and went out back, toward the cabins.

"What?" Less asked.

"I got some very strange flashes back there.

There's something in your cabin, and there's someone else ... involved. Actually the driving force behind whatever else.

"I've never had this kind of confusion with the talent before. It's more than weird!"

Les looked grim. "We have to find whatever it is in my place."

They went to the cabin. Nani stood still, closed her eyes, and slowly revolved. She stopped, and started to go on, then turned back. She pointed to the wall, and said, "There."

There was nothing on the wall, but a couple ,of pictures, one of a sailing ship in high seas, one of an old fighter plane, and one of horses.

Les took the pictures down. The one with the fighter plane had some writing on the back of the picture. RB Turnbull. 6/19/98. #4031.

"Box 4031, Ringold Bank and Trust?" Nani said. "Wasn't that the one that was empty?"

"Yeah. Too little, too late."

"It's not what we're after. I didn't get that feeling.

There was a digital camera behind the horses. Les held up the picture and saw a circle where he could see through, clearly, from behind. There was a solenoid-type of thing hooked to a cell phone that turned the camera on and off. There was a charger for the camera and phone attached.

Les turned the whole thing off, and took the camera out. He opened the battery compartment to see there was an eight G memory stick in the slot. He pressed the "on" button. The script came across the screen: *Memory full*.

"Hmm. Let's see what the last twenty hours of recording shows us!" Nani suggested.

Les took the chip out and inserted it into a card reader. It started with a clip of him taking off his clothes, then a local preacher coming to pet him and grope him. It got a bit too much. Les looked bored.

Next was someone not familiar to them. Much the same.

Then several more in that vein.

Then The Senator – and that one was on the order that, according to Nani, could put his ass away for twenty to life.

"How? I didn't try to stop him, really. He likes to act like he's forcing me, but he wasn't, really. Dominance bit, Mom called it. Kinky, but not unusual."

"Really? And how old were you?"

"About seventeen."

"So you were a legal minor. You were being forced into perverted sex acts by the wonderful senator who's head of the state board on child abuse and pedophilia crimes."

"He didn't really force me."

"Well, it certainly looked like he did! What? The court is to believe their eyes or the word of someone who, noting his bank account figures, was being paid *not* to tell?"

"I don't think that's important, in itself. What I want to know is if he was part of my Mom's murder, if he did it, or if it was Harry.

"If it was Harry, was it because he was forced to kill her?

"I'm further behind than I was when it started!"

"We'll work out something. Maybe with Harry. He doesn't have anything else to lose."

Les looked thoughtful [for real, this time]. He picked up his phone and punched Harry's number.

"Hi. We want to get a few things sorted out. There's nothing to gain for knocking us over, anymore," Les greeted. "It's more for information. We may act on it, or not. It's for my own understanding.

"Is it all from Carstair?"

Harry looked shocked. "How did ... I mean, I don't even talk to him much. Just at the restaurant.

"You should have blown up my cabin. You knew the cameras were there."

"I wasn't sure. I knew they were for awhile, but I thought she'd taken them out.

"It was me, for some of it. Him for some of it. LeSeur was his employee, not mine. He worked for Carstairs, but Maria gave him the orders."

Les tried to not show his shock. Nani saw that, and said, "Harry, I want to do a little thing. It's from my talent.

"You see, I'm a schizophrenic. There really is a Mama Nani. She has some powers. I don't. I usually don't know what she's doing. We have an agreement, where she can act, at times, and I can, at other times.

"Right now, we are communicating. I'll let her take over for a few minutes."

Harry was looking confused and disbelieving.

"Okay now, Mon. I is Mama Nani. I has powers. I can tell when you is lying, and I gets these flashes when you is making plans, like the one a few minutes ago to take out the gun in you back 'n shoot us two, then youself.

"I done think you is guilty maybe one fourth. You is under orders 'n you is hopeless to stop 'em.

"You didn't set off no bomb here. It supposed to get *you*, no others. Did you order Yveth dead?"

"No! I didn't order anyone to be killed. I only told Maria what you said!"

"S'truth. Who kill Yveth?"

"LeSeur."

"From?"

"Carstairs or Maria.

"Mama Nani, Les, I never did anything except tell them what was happening. I did kill someone, and they have the proof. It was a woman who got pregnant to force me to marry her! It was for the money! She didn't love me! She said so when we had an argument, and I went crazy and hit her, then she tried to stab me with an ice pick, and I strangled her! I tried to stop, but I couldn't!

"Carstairs and Maria were somehow behind it. They had pictures of me killing her. They made me do everything since."

"S'truth.

"Harry, I done got powers. I done got an idee we can get them to hell, right fast.

"Mama Nani done got to talk to them, in person, like. Mama Nani can see they gets to each one t'other. What you done called poets justice. Mama Nani sees what am to happen. It be clear."

"What'll you do?" Les asked.

"I done let them be what they is. What you calls their natural nature."

"How can I get them to talk to you?" Harry asked.

"They done scairt of you. Real scairt! They

doesn't want you to never know that. You can tell 'em they talks to me or a video thing is gonna accidently end up on the World Bank investigator desk."

"Maria knows there aren't any World Bank investigators here," Harry warned.

"Naw, Mon. She done *think* they ain't here. She done scairt they is. The Senator done know they's them videos. He ain't no problem."

"I'll do whatever you say. I think I'd rather be dead than to live this way anymore."

"Well then! How's about we get this boat in the water, Mon!"

They made their plans. It would be at eight tonight, at Goofy's, which was closed for repairs.

When they were on their way back to Nani's house to get ready, after putting a few little items in their special places, Les asked, "Is the schizophrenic thing real?"

"Yes and no. It's a sort of theatrical act I started, and it's become part of me. I can turn over the control to either."

He nodded. "I hope this works."

"Mama Nani do have powers. It be like she see."

Les gave her the finger. She laughed. "It's true though. I do have the power to see."

"I'm glad you had the sense to come here," Les said to Maria and Carstairs. "You are in a really bad spot. Both of you, and, in both cases, one of you can save the other's hide. It's only a matter of which one, and if you will.

"Miss Estevez, you ordered the death of Yveth Tatum. We have proof. Carstairs, you are a pedophile who preys on eight and ten year old boys. We have proof."

"You have no such thing!" Maria snarled. "That's absurd!"

"LeSeur had a conversation with us before he met his timely demise. We're not here to argue about that. Our concern is about what has happened since that time."

"He didn't give you anything about *me*!" she spat.

"He was a semi-professional hit man. He hedged his bets.

"Senator, you are perfectly well-aware that Yveth had videos of your little escapades with me, her son.

"I didn't know about that until recently.

"That she's dead doesn't really bother me. We were never close, in the family way. She was like the madam, and I was one of the whores.

"We did get along. Very well. There were times I felt some affection for her, and times I believe she felt for me.

"This is about something else. A duplicity. It concerns one or both of you. You brought yourselves into it, solidly, when you tried to steal my inheritance.

"If you hadn't done that, you might have gone on for some time. It was the mistake that has to be corrected."

"Wait a moment, here," Carstairs demanded. "What is this duplicity you speak of?"

"Please!

"You know Mama Nani. We've all met. I'll let her determine where the blame lies in this silliness."

"You will not bring some fake witch into this! No one would believe you for a minute!" Maria cried. "We are wasting our time here, Senator. I, for one, am leaving!"

"Without finding out if the senator is the duplicitous one?" Harry said, from the corner, out of sight, until they turned to see him. "I think, just perhaps, we have an answer?

"Senator, I think you have a lot to lose here. I'm trying to see that certain videos are *not* preserved. They are the only reason you are not in the jails you're so intent in seeing others held."

Carstairs, who was just starting to stand, slumped back in his chair.

"Well ... get this farce over with! I have things to do!" Maria snarled [She snarled a lot.]

"Mama Nani?" Les said.

She came from the small room to the side, stood still a moment, turned to face Maria, shook her head, and turned to Carstairs.

"You done both be deceivers."

"Well, now we get the voodoo bit!" Maria spat. "Do you think I'm stupid?"

"You is. That ain't no real actual part 'n this."

"Oh? Really? Is that all you've got?"

"I done got the flash!" [For Les.]

"I done seed you two year past. You is at a place ... with water outside and under.

"A boat?"

"No. A ... log house in the water. Over the water. You is with a man. George? Kevin? Real young, but look older.

"Kevin. The man done got handsome, a lot like Les, but different. Him got blond hair. Him got a body like a god. Him is ... you ... son of car driver man. Him is seventeen years old. Him is like sex with you. Him say he done got ... done got ... somethin' from you safe in the wall at you house.

"He don't want nothin'! He like you! You done kilt him for nothin'! He think it not real!"

Maria was wide-eyed, and was shaking.

"It's not true! I never ... No one could know ...

It's a lie!"

"The police done got fingerprints them don't know for who. They got DNA they don't know for who.

"You is done. We doesn't need no more, Les.

"Now, Senator. We done got the videos. You done through, too.

"I done seed what's to happen. It not can change. We is all what we is.

"Harry, you done seed hell. You done right, this time, 'n you have absolution, but you bees careful o you is right back there.

"These two done got hell they deserves comin' right fast. Senator have chance to change. She don't. She live in hell here, then she die and go to other hell.

"Les, you'n me gets what we deserves, too. I see you'n Mama Nani, well, Nani, on a boat, lookin' at the water in the sea near Italy. You is in a place with lots of statues. You is on a island with lots of coconuts. You is getting older, and you is considerin' havin' some kids, but not if you ... I no can read past.

"Les, let's go home. This is as far as we go here. Maria will turn on Carstairs, and he will turn on her. They will both spend the rest of their lives in jail."

"Sounds like a plan. My questions are answered,

so I'm free!"

Everyone else was staring at each other as they left. Harry sighed, and said he was going home. Carstairs and Maria glared at each other.

Each to his own path.

Natalie and Lee Tatum waved at their parents, then got on the plane that would take them to their scholarships at UC Berkeley. Les put the camera in its sack, hugged Nani, and went to their car to drive back to the cabin on the bay.

"You know, Mother, I think we did a fairly good job as parents. I'm damned proud of you, and don't care who knows it!"

She grinned her impish grin at him. They stopped at the old restaurant where they first worked together. They would celebrate their 55th and 54th birthday there. They were three days apart, on the calendar, so they would celebrate the day between, as they had done for years.

The old grizzled owner came to greet them. He had a special table prepared for them.

"Well, Harry, can I spend an hour in the cabin in back with a ten year old boy I met?" Les asked.

"His mother raised the price to two hundred. She wants to see he gets a good inheritance."

They laughed and joked. Harry said they needed a bartender, and heard Les had some experience in that.

"Well, I'll see if I can make it a little longer. My bank account's down to just two million, so I want to start putting a bit aside for when I retire."

"Had anymore bombs in the kitchen" Nani asked.

"Not since that conch chowder Emile put on the menu."

They sat on the deck to watch the pinks and golds of the magnificent sunset.

"Y'know, Hon? I think we done good."

He kissed her hair.

C. D. Moulton's works are available on most major outlets as printed or e-books. CD writes the CD Grimes, PI, mysteries, the Det. Lt. Nick Storie mysteries, the Clint Faraday mysteries, the Flight of the Maita science fiction series, books on orchid culture and many others of many types. Mystery, adventure, intrigue, science fiction, humor, fantasy, paranormal, mild erotica, and factual.